Where is Tatum's Voice?

Our Journey with Childhood Apraxia of Speech

Written by Bridget Tippett

Illustrated by Jeremy Provost

LITTLE CREEK PRESS®
AND BOOK DESIGN

Mineral Point, Wisconsin USA

Little Creek Press®
A Division of Kristin Mitchell Design, Inc.
5341 Sunny Ridge Road
Mineral Point, Wisconsin 53565

Book Design and Project Coordination:
Little Creek Press

First Edition
September 2019

Printed in Wisconsin, United States of America

To order books visit www.littlecreekpress.com

Library of Congress Control Number: 2019910755

ISBN-13: 978-1-942586-63-0

Tatum

To our baby girl, may you dream big, princess,
and use your voice to inspire the world.

Jack

To our little man, thank you for your patience
and being Tatum's voice when she needs it.

Aunt Jean

Thank you for teaching me to read at a
young age and for my love of books.

When we found out Tatum was diagnosed with childhood apraxia of speech, we were heartbroken and defeated. We didn't know where to begin to understand and help Tatum with this rare disorder. After much research, we found Tatum's first speech therapist, an amazing speech and language pathologist named Leslie Bennett. She was our shoulder to cry on, our ray of sunshine on the toughest of days, and the reassuring voice telling us that everything would be okay. She has been a blessing to our family.

Thank you to our family and friends for their neverending support and help. We want to especially thank our parents, Steve and Jane Cleary and LaVerne and Elaine Tippett. Thank you for the endless support, guidance, prayers, and time spent driving to and from appointments, watching the kids, and always listening to our struggles and joys. Thank you for always being there for us.

Thank you to my husband, Dan, who allows me to be a dreamer and accomplish my dream of being a children's book author. His continuous support, love, and gentle ways on the darkest days make life much brighter. Tatum is beyond blessed to be "your little girl." Love you forever and ever.

To Jack and Tatum, the best children God could have blessed me with. Tatum, despite having apraxia, you are the most amazing, hardworking, and beautiful girl. Your determination makes me keep fighting, and you inspire me every day. Jack, you are the most kindhearted, creative, and sweetest boy I know. I love how much you love Tatum and are so thankful she has you as her big brother. I love you both to the moon and back! ♥

To the reader,

I have wanted to write a book for quite some time. When Tatum was diagnosed with apraxia, I knew this would be the topic of my book. When I started writing, the words flowed so easily, as this is our life—our journey. I wrote this book to raise awareness about this rare neurological speech and motor disorder. Apraxia occurs in only 1 out of 1,000 (less than 1%) of children. I hope by reading this book, you gain knowledge and understand this invisible disorder. I believe every child deserves a voice and will use it to create a kinder and better world!

Kindly,
Bridget Tippett

" Raising a child with apraxia is truly a blessing. It has taught me to slow down, enjoy the small moments, and celebrate the baby steps. It has made me cry happy tears over the smallest bit of progress, such as saying a new word. It has also made me cry sad tears over the frustration of not being able to understand what our daughter wants or needs as she is crying out in frustration. This lifelong apraxia journey we are on is so challenging some days. However, it has a unique beauty of its own; you just have to see it through the eyes of a child with apraxia."

Bridget Tippett

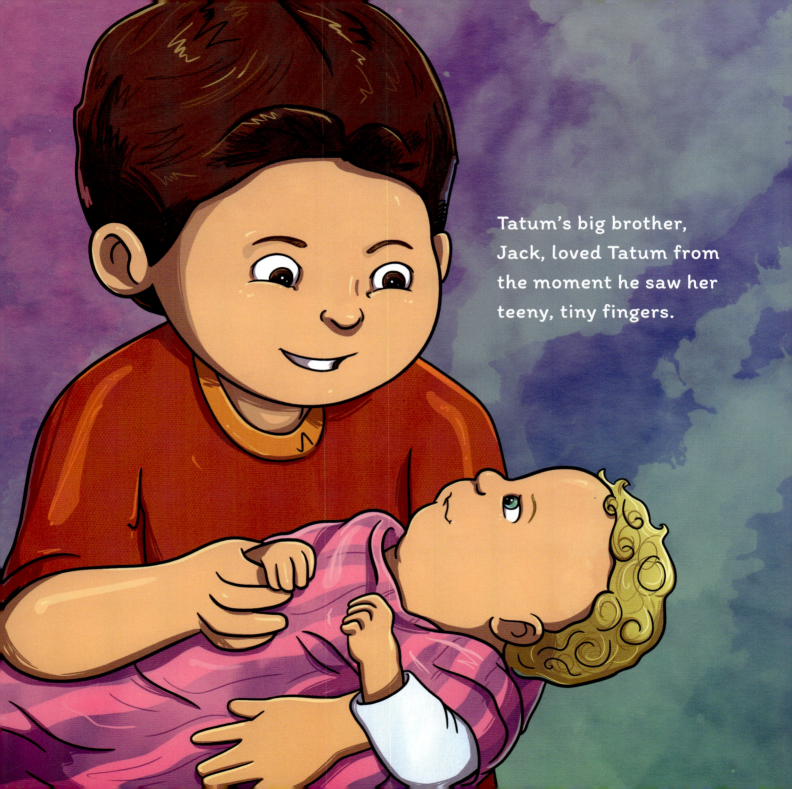

Tatum's big brother, Jack, loved Tatum from the moment he saw her teeny, tiny fingers.

As she grew from a baby to a toddler, Jack couldn't wait for Tatum to talk. As Tatum got older, Jack couldn't understand why she would make noises to "talk" instead of using words like he did.

Jack started to wonder why Tatum wasn't talking. She looked like all the other kids her age. She could color, play hide and seek, put together puzzles, and act silly. Where was Tatum's voice?

Tatum's mom and dad wondered this too, and became worried. Tatum was frustrated that her parents and brother couldn't understand what she was telling them.

They took Tatum to a speech therapist who listened to her try to talk and tested her. Then they met with doctors who did even more tests. Those tests showed that Tatum was born with childhood apraxia of speech.

Childhood apraxia of speech is a speech disorder that starts in the brain. This means that it is very difficult for the brain, jaw, mouth and tongue to work together at the same time to produce sounds and words.

People may have a difficult time understanding children with apraxia. Children with apraxia can become discouraged because people cannot understand what they want or need.

Even though they may not be able to say the words correctly, their brains know exactly what words should come out.

There is no cure for apraxia. Hearing those words was confusing for her mom and dad because, at first, they didn't know how to help their little girl.

Tatum's mom and dad understood that this disorder wasn't going away, and they decided to do EVERYTHING they could to help her.

Her mom and dad learned everything they could about apraxia, raised money for research and resources, and met with other parents whose children have apraxia.

After a lot of speech therapy, tears, frustration, prayers, patience, and hard work, Tatum is slowly finding her voice!

Through lots of hard work and practice, Tatum went from speaking in simple, single words to telling funny jokes, sharing secrets with Jack, telling long stories, and singing silly songs.

Tatum can dance, ride her bike, play games,
and play with their dog Rudy and Jack outside.

Tatum makes friends at school where
her teachers and classmates
understand and support her.

Even though Tatum will always struggle with her words, her mom and dad would like her to one day have a voice of her own where people of all ages can understand her needs and wants.

Tatum's family is blessed that she has so many important people in her life who support and love her and show her patience as she continues to find and use her voice.

About Childhood Apraxia of Speech

Childhood apraxia of speech (CAS) is a motor speech disorder that makes it hard for children to speak. Children with the diagnosis of apraxia of speech generally have a good understanding of language and know what they want to say. However, they have difficulty learning or carrying out the complex movements that underlie speech.

Apraxia of speech has been called verbal apraxia, developmental apraxia of speech, or verbal dyspraxia. The most commonly used term used today is childhood apraxia of speech. No matter what name is used, the most important concept is the root word "praxis." Praxis means planned movement. To some degree or another, a child with the diagnosis of apraxia of speech has difficulty programming and planning speech movements. Apraxia of speech is a specific speech disorder. This difficulty in planning speech movements is the hallmark or "signature" of childhood apraxia of speech.

The challenge and difficulty that children with apraxia have in creating speech can seem very perplexing to parents, especially when they observe the skill of learning to speak developing seemingly without effort in other children.

The top three characteristics of childhood apraxia of speech, as reported by the American Speech-Language-Hearing Association (ASHA) Technical Report on Childhood Apraxia of Speech, that can help the SLP make a differential diagnosis are:

- Inconsistent errors with consonants and vowels on repeated productions of syllables and words. (Your child says the same word in different ways when asked to repeat it several times. This might be more apparent in new words or longer more complex words.)

- Difficulty moving from sound to sound or syllable to syllable, resulting in lengthened pauses between sounds and/or syllables

- Inappropriate stress on syllables or words (such as all syllables are said with equal stress on each one causing the "melody" of speech to sound odd)

For more information on apraxia, go to www.apraxia-kids.org

Information courtesy: www.apraxia-kids.org

Apraxia Kids Organization

A portion of the proceeds from this book will benefit Apraxia Kids. Apraxia Kids is the leading nonprofit organization that strengthens the support systems in the lives of children with apraxia of speech by educating professionals and families, facilitating community engagement and outreach, and investing in the future through advocacy and research. Their vision is a world where every child with apraxia of speech reaches their highest communication potential through accurate diagnosis and appropriate, timely treatment. ♥

About the Author

Advocate, teacher, wife, and mom, Bridget Tippett, is beyond blessed to have written her first book. She feels strongly that every child deserves a voice and is passionate about being an apraxia advocate for her daughter, Tatum, and other children who are diagnosed with this rare neurological speech and motor disorder. Bridget, her husband Dan, their children, Jack, and Tatum, and their dog Rudy live in southwest Wisconsin. ♥